CONTENTS

1. Christmas Is Coming   5

2. Playing Around   19

3. Missing Jesus   30

4. Rhymes from the Kidnapper   40

5. Silent Night   47

6. Gingerbread but No Answers   56

7. Christmas Secrets   65

8. Snow Day   74

9. Another Day, Another Poem   80

10. A Late Start to the Season   86

11. The Eve of Christmas Eve   96

12. A Christmas Miracle   109

13. The Greatest Gift   113

A Christmas Play   122

D0127093

1 CHRISTMAS IS COMING

"Mikey, what are you doing?" Elizabeth demanded. "I thought you were going to help me."

"I thought I told you not to call me Mikey," Elizabeth's younger brother answered, not looking up. Mike was lying on his stomach, studying a brightly colored Christmas catalog.

Elizabeth snatched the book out from under his nose. "Hey!" Mike said, scrambling up to his hands and knees.

"Christmas is next week," said Elizabeth. "We have a tree with no decorations, and the outdoor Nativity set is still in the garage. I'm supposed to be working on a play for youth group, and you're looking at a catalog!" She threw it across the room.

Mike sat on his heels, looking at the catalog, then at his sister.

Elizabeth stood in the middle of the living room, her hands at her sides, fists clenched, fighting back tears. This was one of the worst Christmases yet. The worst had been the first Christmas after Dad died. No one had felt like celebrating, although going to church that Christmas Eve had started the healing in her heart and in her mom's and in Mike's. Hearing the story of Jesus' birth to be their Savior had given them hope and comfort. This year it wasn't sadness interfering with the preparations, it was busyness.

"When's Mom coming back?" Mike asked, his lower lip quivering.

Elizabeth saw tears glistening in his eyes. "I'm sorry," she said, retrieving the catalog and handing it to her brother. "You don't remember what a big deal it was to Dad to set up the Nativity. It belonged to his mom and dad, our grandma and grandpa, you know."

Mike smoothed the pages of the catalog, then placed it on top of the list he'd been printing. "We don't have any presents yet either," he said, looking at the bare floor under the equally bare tree in the corner.

"Mom's really busy with the giving tree at church. It'll be over soon," Elizabeth reminded him. Mom and Aunt Nan, who lived in the other side of their duplex and was like a grandmother to them, were co-chairing a project collecting Christmas gifts for needy families. Even Mom said it was taking more time than she'd expected. Their family Christmas plans were on hold, but it was hard to be mad at Mom for doing something good. It wasn't hard, Elizabeth corrected herself, it just made her feel bad that she resented the time her mother was giving to help people who had so little. Wasn't that the true spirit of Christmas, sharing Jesus' love with others?

"Would you help me set up the Nativity?" Elizabeth asked Mike, nicely this time.

"I guess. Mom isn't here to help me write

my letter to Santa anyway. She said we'd do it today. If we don't get it in the mail soon, he might not get it in time," said Mike, a frown causing his eyebrows to almost meet over his nose.

"If you help me with the Nativity, I'll help you write a letter to Santa," Elizabeth promised.

The wrinkles in Mike's forehead disappeared. "You will? What do you want me to do?"

"I already have the stable set up." Elizabeth moved to the front window and pointed at the rough, three-sided wooden structure she'd struggled with most of the afternoon. "You can put straw down while I carry the people out." She'd already done all the hard work, but she wanted Mike to share the fun of setting up the rest of the scene.

Mike opened the front door. "Don't forget your coat," said Elizabeth. It was warm for December, but not that warm. Another reason, she thought, that it was hard to get in the spirit of the season.

In the garage, Elizabeth lifted the statue of Joseph out of the protective carton where he spent most of the year. She took an old towel and carefully dusted him off, rubbing the painted plaster until he shined. The figure was heavy, but she managed to get him to the front yard.

"That looks great," Elizabeth said. Mike had spread straw under the stable roof and around the outside of the wooden structure. "Save the rest," she added. She set Joseph upright in the stable.

A black Volvo pulled into the driveway, a big red bow on the front of the car and a smaller red bow on the radio antenna. The man behind the wheel gave a short toot of the horn.

"Don!" Mike yelled and waved. He turned to Elizabeth and added, "He can help too."

Elizabeth waited for Don Hamilton to get out of the car. The old reluctance to include her mom's soon-to-be husband in their family traditions reared its head. After all, the Nativity had been her dad's. It seemed like she was the only one in the family who felt reluctant to share traditions with Don. But even as she wanted to protect the old ways, Elizabeth had to admit that she liked Don more than she thought she ever would.

"Where's your mother?" Don asked, joining them.

"At church," said Elizabeth. "We decided we'd put some decorations out since our house is the only one on the street without any."

Tiger, Elizabeth's orange-striped cat, jumped off the porch and wrapped himself around Don's legs. Don patted him on the head.

"Is there anything I can do?" Don asked.

Elizabeth's first impulse was to say no, but she quickly swallowed it. "Would you hook up the spotlight? There's a long cord in the garage. It plugs into the outlet on the porch."

"No problem," said Don, smiling. "Point me to the light and cord."

Elizabeth headed toward the garage, Mike, Don, and Tiger tagging along behind. She pulled the light and cord from one of the boxes marked "Christmas Decorations."

While Don untangled the extension cord, with help from Mike, Elizabeth took Mary out of her carton. She carefully cleaned the caked dirt out of the folds of Mary's blue robe. Elizabeth loved the color the robe was painted.

"Look at all these," Mike said.

Elizabeth turned to see him holding a tangle of multi-colored Christmas lights. "Put those away. We haven't put them up in years." Since Dad died, she added to herself.

"Don't they work anymore?" Don asked.

"It's not that," said Elizabeth. "We just haven't ... we don't ... Mom didn't ..."

"Do you want to hang them? What about outside?" asked Don.

"Yeah!" Mike jumped around the garage, clapping his hands. "I'll bet there are a million jillion lights here. Our house will be brighter than anybody's."

"There are a lot," said Don, pulling out more.

Elizabeth turned back to Mary. It's okay, she thought. He's part of the family ... almost.

11

While Don and Mike worked on the lights, Elizabeth carried Mary to the stable and placed her beside Joseph.

Returning to the garage, Elizabeth took the manger from the hook where it had hung since last Christmas. "Can you come fill this with straw?" she asked Mike.

"I'm helping Don," Mike said.

Again Elizabeth bit back what she really wanted to say and said nothing instead. It was Christmas, right? she reminded herself. After she placed the manger between Mary and Joseph, she heaped it full of straw, making a place to lay the baby.

Mike and Don were singing Christmas songs when she returned to the garage. Elizabeth found herself humming "Jingle Bells" in spite of herself.

She opened the last carton and baby Jesus smiled up at her, his lips red and his cheeks pink. This was the happiest baby Jesus she'd ever seen. Most Nativity babies were solemn, but her Jesus looked like he was happy to be born as her

Savior. Every time she looked at him, Elizabeth was happy the real Jesus had been born.

"Anybody home? I heard the music and thought maybe I was missing a party."

"Hi, Justin," said Elizabeth, smiling broadly. Having Justin stop by made her feel even more festive. She held baby Jesus for him to see.

"Who's that?" Justin asked.

Elizabeth couldn't believe her ears. She cradled Jesus in her arms. "It's the Christ Child," she said.

"Doesn't look like him," Justin mumbled, his fair cheeks turning bright red.

"This one looks a little different," said Don. "Looks more like one of Santa's elves."

Elizabeth opened her mouth, then snapped it shut. Her baby Jesus did have a twinkle of mischief in his eye. It was one of the things she liked about him.

"Justin, you help my man Mike untangle these lights while I go around front and see how many we need," said Don, clapping Justin on the back. Pointing at baby Jesus, he asked Elizabeth,

"Want me to carry that?"

Elizabeth shook her head.

"Tell me how you want the lights," Don said, walking with Elizabeth to the front of the house.

"We used to put them across the porch, over Aunt Nan's too," said Elizabeth, picturing Dad on the ladder hanging the strands of lights.

"Did you ever wrap them around the porch railing?" asked Don.

"Nope," said Elizabeth.

"Around the doors? the windows?"

She shook her head.

"There's a lot of lights for just the porch," said Don.

Elizabeth laughed. "Not all of them work. When one strand didn't light up, Dad just bought another."

"It's probably just a burned out bulb," said Don.

Elizabeth shrugged. It was Dad's way.

"Well, by replacing some bulbs, we can light up this house like you've never seen it," said

14

Don, rubbing his hands together.

"Don't forget the spotlight for the Nativity," said Elizabeth.

Don rubbed baby Jesus' head. "Don't worry," he said.

Elizabeth turned to place the figure in the manger. "Listen," said Don, catching her arm, "I need some help with a present. For your mother."

"She'll like anything you buy her," said Elizabeth.

"But I want something special."

"One thing she'd like is to see you at church," said Elizabeth.

Don sighed. "I know."

"There's a special service on Christmas Eve. Mike will be singing, and I'll be in a play. Mom will be sitting alone."

"I'll think about it," said Don, staring at baby Jesus. "But I was thinking about jewelry or perfume—something like that."

Elizabeth settled baby Jesus in his bed of straw. The family looked happy to be together again. Justin and Mike came around the corner of the house dragging strings of lights behind them.

"Let me get a ladder, and we'll start hanging these babies," said Don.

"Better test them first," said Elizabeth.

"Good idea." He winked at her.

Another car pulled up, and the door opened. "What time is it?" Elizabeth asked, watching her friend, Christy, get out of the car and wave as her mother drove away.

"Ten to three," said Justin. Elizabeth groaned.

"You sound glad to see me," said Christy.

"I forgot about the meeting," said Elizabeth. She turned to Justin and Don. "Will one of you stay with Mike until Mom or Aunt Nan gets home?"

"We have a pizza party for my Scout troop at five. I have to take a present," said Mike, the tiny frown lines reappearing between his eyes.

"We'll make sure you have a present," said Don.

"Wrapped?" asked Mike.

"Wrapped. And we'll make sure you're there on time," Don added. He asked Elizabeth, "Do you need a ride?"

"If I'd known your mother wasn't going to be here, my mom could have dropped us off," said Christy. "But you said she'd be going to church anyway."

"I know, but she went earlier than I expected." Elizabeth calculated—by the time she gathered the play parts and they walked to church, the meeting would have started.

"C'mon. I'll drive you," said Don.

"Five minutes?" asked Elizabeth.

"When you're ready. Meanwhile, I'll get my helpers started on testing the lights. When you get home, you'd better be wearing shades!" said Don.

"I'll help too, as long as I'm here," said Christy, moving closer to Justin. "What do you want me to do?"

Elizabeth ran inside and up to her room. She grabbed her play notes and her Bible, pausing in front of the mirror. Her long, red hair was in a tangle from being outside most of the afternoon, but there wasn't a brush in sight. She did the best she could with her fingers, then sped back down the stairs to the porch, then into Don's car.

Shouldn't preparing for the birth of Jesus be a little less hectic? Elizabeth asked herself.

2

PLAYING AROUND

"A living Nativity," said Elizabeth, wrinkling her nose. "How many years have we done a living Nativity for the Christmas Eve service?"

"People expect it," said Christy. "What would Christmas be without kids dressed as Mary and Joseph, shepherds and angels?"

"I want to do something more," Elizabeth said.

"Like what?" asked Ms. Clark, throwing out the hard question.

Elizabeth had been looking forward for months to planning the Christmas Eve church service with her youth group. She wanted it to be something different—something special— something that would make people think about what Christmas truly means. She'd also hoped that someone else would come up with an idea, but in case no one else did, she had some notes.

Elizabeth chewed on her lower lip. She looked at the group sitting in a semicircle at one end of the church hall. There were eighth-graders at one end of the half-moon of chairs, sitting with arms folded and eyes glazed, not saying a word. There were sixth-graders at the other end, listening, but not saying a word.

"Any suggestions?" Ms. Clark asked again. She looked at Elizabeth. "If not ..."

"A play." The words came out before Elizabeth could stop them. She dropped her head, her long red hair creating a shield between her and her neighbors, hiding the blush she could feel creeping up her neck and into her cheeks. She heard a few whispers and snickers at the end of the row and a loud sigh from Christy, a fellow seventh-grader.

"A play. Sounds like a fine idea, but I'm not sure if we have enough time," said Ms. Clark.

"I like it," said Meghan.

"You would," mumbled Christy.

Elizabeth smiled a *thanks* to her best friend.

Ms. Clark's eyes darted from person to person. She cleared her throat. "Any ideas about what the play should be about?"

"The birth of Jesus," said Christy at the same time Elizabeth said, "Finding the meaning of Christmas."

"The birth of Jesus is the true meaning of Christmas," Christy said, smiling smugly.

"But people forget," Elizabeth said, thinking about how she'd spent the day preparing for Christmas but not for the coming of Christ.

"I have an idea," Meghan said, her quiet voice cutting across Elizabeth's and Christy's rising voices. Both girls and Ms. Clark turned to her.

"It's too silly," Meghan said, grabbing the end of her dark braid and brushing it back and forth across her lips.

"C'mon," said Elizabeth, her eyes pleading with Meghan to come up with something new.

"We're open to everything," added Ms. Clark.

Studying the end of the braid, Meghan took a deep breath. "What about a play about the birth of Jesus?"

"You mean have Mary and Joseph, the angels and shepherds, talk?" asked Christy.

"Well," said Meghan. "I'm not sure …"

Elizabeth felt a tingle. It started in her stomach and traveled up to the base of her skull. She had it! "Instead of Bethlehem, Mary and Joseph find themselves here, today. Everybody they meet and ask for help is too busy. But at the end, we can have a live Nativity!" She said it so quickly that the words bumped into one another, becoming one long word.

Christy stared at Elizabeth for a long moment, then she nodded her head. Several other people also were smiling and nodding.

"Any volunteers to write a play?" Ms. Clark asked.

Christy's and Elizabeth's hands shot into the air. With a little help from Elizabeth, Meghan's followed more slowly. "Great!" said Ms. Clark. "You know we don't have much time?"

The girls nodded.

"For the rest of the group, we need scenery and costumes. But let's keep it simple," said Ms. Clark. The youth-group leader assigned everyone to a group.

"We'll need to get started on this play now," said Elizabeth, "or we won't have time to finish it *and* practice."

"I can do it quickly," said Christy.

"And I'll work fast too," said Elizabeth.

"How about tonight?" Christy asked.

Elizabeth wasn't sure what Mom had planned. Mike was at his pizza party, but Justin had been at her house when she left. On Saturday nights he often came by to watch a movie or play games. "What about tomorrow afternoon?"

"My mom and I are going to bake Christmas cookies," said Christy. "Why? What are you doing tonight?" Since Christy had been caught shoplifting earlier in the year, her old group of friends had dropped her. Now she often tried to join Elizabeth and Meghan. It wasn't that she didn't like Christy, Elizabeth thought, but it was different having another person around.

"We can do it tonight, I guess," said Elizabeth. She turned to Meghan. "Can you come?"

"I thought we'd be watching a movie anyway. What about Justin and Rich, though?" Meghan asked.

"If you already have plans ..." Christy began, looking at the floor between her feet.

"It's nothing formal. Come over about six, and we'll have pizza and get right to work," said Elizabeth.

Christy shook her head, the ends of her straight brown hair whipping back and forth across her face.

"C'mon," said Elizabeth, starting to feel bad for Christy.

"Elizabeth!" Mom's voice interrupted. "Where's Mike?"

"He's at the house with Don and Justin," said Elizabeth. "He said he has a party with the Scouts ..."

Mom gasped and covered her mouth with her hand. "He's supposed to take a present."

"Relax, Mom. Don said he'd take care of it."

"Wow, Mrs. Bryan, you're pretty lucky to have a boyfriend like Mr. Hamilton," said Christy.

"*Blessed* is the word," said Mom. "He probably thinks I've forgotten all about his faculty party tonight. You'll be home, won't you, to watch Mike?"

"We were going to work on our play," said Elizabeth.

"What kind of trouble are you planning?" asked Aunt Nan, joining them.

"You can come over to my house," Christy said. "No, you have to watch your little brother."

"You can come to Elizabeth's, and I'll come over and keep order," said Aunt Nan.

"Can we order pizza?" asked Elizabeth.

"I'll do one better and make spaghetti," said Aunt Nan.

"I'll be there," said Meghan.

"Are you ready to come now?" asked Mom.

"That's a great idea. Then we can get started before dinner," said Elizabeth. "Call your moms and find out."

"I can call from your house," said Christy.

"Me too," said Meghan. "I was planning on getting a ride home with you anyway."

"I'll meet you at the car," said Mom. "I have to get my purse."

Elizabeth found the car parked near the door. The girls got in the backseat. "So, is Justin still at your house?" Christy asked, checking her hair in the rearview mirror.

"I'm not sure," said Elizabeth, although she knew he probably was. Deliberately changing the subject, Elizabeth added, "Let's start the play with Mary and Joseph walking down a town street."

"What will they wear?" asked Christy. "Clothes like today or their regular clothes, you know, bathrobes?"

"Robes," said Meghan. "What stores should we have?"

"A bakery where they're too busy baking cookies to help," said Christy.

"A card shop where they're selling and

addressing Christmas cards?" suggested Elizabeth.

"Christmas cards?" Mom groaned as she slid into the driver's seat. "That's something else I haven't done yet."

"Stop worrying about what you haven't done," said Aunt Nan. "You're doing something wonderful with the giving tree, something for Jesus."

Mom backed the car out of the parking space and headed home. It was hard to write with the car moving, but Elizabeth couldn't wait. The words were running through her brain so quickly that she could barely move her pencil across the page fast enough.

"Oh, my!" Mom said as she pulled into the driveway behind Don's car.

"It's awesome!" said Meghan.

"Fantastic!" Christy said.

Aunt Nan and Elizabeth stared silently at the blaze of lights. There were lights across the roof, around the doors and windows, wrapped around the porch railing and posts. It looks like a foil-wrapped Christmas gift, thought Elizabeth.

"Do you like it?" Don asked as he opened Mom's car door.

"It's pretty amazing," said Mom.

Justin was standing on the sidewalk, looking at the house through a camera. "This lens works," he shouted to Don. "But I'm still not sure how to set the f-stop."

"I didn't know Justin took pictures," said Christy.

"Don is teaching him," said Elizabeth.

"They take so many pictures they're almost irritating," Meghan added.

"I wouldn't mind," said Christy. "I have a new camera, so maybe he can give me some hints."

"One student at a time may be all Don can handle," said Elizabeth, knowing that wasn't who Christy wanted to ask for hints.

As Elizabeth stepped out of the car, she noticed that the one dark place in the yard was the spot she'd specifically asked Don to light.

"Where's the spotlight for the Nativity?"

"I didn't forget," said Don. "I only forgot to turn it on." He jogged to the porch and plugged in the cord.

The light came on and the Nativity came to life—almost. "Wait a minute," said Elizabeth. "Who kidnapped Jesus?"

3

MISSING JESUS

Everyone crowded around the manger. "Don? Justin? Where is he?" Elizabeth asked, smiling at the joke.

"I don't know," said Don, moving closer.

"Me either," said Justin, snapping a picture of the empty manger. "But there's something there."

Elizabeth grabbed the piece of white paper stuck in the hay. She read the message aloud:

> *Don't worry about foul play.*
> *I've gone but not too far away.*
> *There's things to see I haven't seen.*
> *There's things to do I haven't done.*
> *It's Christmas time. Let's all have fun.*
> *In your heart, I'll always be.*
> *Prepare and wait to welcome me.*

Elizabeth looked at Don, then Justin. "Okay,

the joke's over. Where is he?"

"Isn't that always the question?" asked Aunt Nan.

"He'll turn up," said Don, putting his arm around Elizabeth. "Maybe it isn't time yet."

"Mom!"

"I'm sure it must be a joke," said Mom.

"It's not funny," said Elizabeth, looking at Don and Justin again.

"Everyone go on in, and I'll have dinner before long. No one is going to put him back while we're standing here gawking. Lydia, you have a party to go to, and I'll bet Justin is hungry," said Aunt Nan.

"Always," said Justin, picking up his large black gym bag and tucking the camera inside. He followed Aunt Nan into the house.

"Great tree," Christy said as Elizabeth gathered their coats and piled them on the steps.

"Maybe you should have saved some lights for it," said Meghan.

"We're going to decorate it tomorrow," said Elizabeth. "The branches need to fall out, you know, after they've been squashed at the tree lot." No one needed to know it had been sitting there since last Sunday.

"I'll pick up Mike and be back for you around seven," Don said to Mom. "You like the decorations, right?"

"I love them. It's been too long since we've had the house decorated," said Mom, kissing Don lightly on the lips.

Elizabeth's face grew warm. What was Mom thinking of, kissing Don in front of her friends? She entered the living room where Justin was snapping pictures of the bare tree.

Christy moved in front of the camera. When it clicked, she turned toward Justin, her eyes wide. "I didn't get in the picture, did I?" she asked.

Justin tucked the camera back into the bag. "I have plenty of others," he said.

"You guys better call your parents," Elizabeth reminded Christy and Meghan. The girls went to use the phone in the kitchen.

"How long is she going to be here?" Justin

asked, nodding toward Christy.

"We have to write a play for Christmas Eve," said Elizabeth.

"You're getting kind of a late start, aren't you?" asked Justin.

"I think everybody thought we'd do a live Nativity again, but I wanted to do something else," said Elizabeth. "And as you just pointed out, we don't have much time."

"You would want to do something else." Justin tugged at a strand of Elizabeth's hair and grinned at her. "You want me to disappear?"

"You can stay and help," said Elizabeth.

"Me? What's the play about?"

"Mary and Joseph and getting ready for Christmas," said Elizabeth.

"You know I don't know anything about that stuff," said Justin.

"That's why you should stay. And we're having Aunt Nan's spaghetti."

"I'll stay." Justin draped himself over an easy chair. "I think Rich is planning to bring a movie over around seven."

"If we're not done with the play, you guys can watch it."

"Watch what?" Christy asked, perching herself on the arm of Justin's chair.

"Nothing," said Justin.

Aunt Nan appeared in the doorway. "You." She pointed at Justin, and he sat up. "Come help me with the salad and let the girls work."

Justin jumped up and hurried into the kitchen. Christy slid into the chair. Elizabeth put her feet on the coffee table, resting her notebook on her knees. "This is what I've got so far," she said. "Mary and Joseph enter and walk toward the town."

"Mom said I can stay." Meghan plopped down beside Elizabeth, crunching on a piece of celery.

"Okay, what town?" asked Christy.

"A modern town," said Elizabeth.

"How are we going to make that?" Meghan asked.

"Paint it on cardboard," said Elizabeth. "Tomorrow at church I'll tell Ms. Clark what stores we need, and she can get the scenery people busy."

"Now, how does this sound? Mary says, 'Joseph, is this Bethlehem?' He says, 'Bethlehem is much different than Nazareth.' They'll be looking all around.

"Mary says, 'I'm tired. Let's get something to eat and find a place to stay.' She takes Joseph's arm."

"Shouldn't we be typing this?" Christy asked.

"I can type it later," said Elizabeth.

"You don't have to do it all," said Christy.

"Let me finish telling you what I've written, then each of you can write some scenes, okay?"

"Go on," said Meghan. Christy folded her arms.

"Mary and Joseph stop in front of a bakery, and Joseph asks, 'Are you hungry?' Mary says, 'You must ask?' and pats her stomach. Joseph says, 'We can get some bread in here.' Inside the baker is decorating Christmas cookies. Mary says, 'Those are pretty. What are they?' The baker looks at her like she's crazy. Joseph says, 'We would like some bread.' The baker says, 'We're out of bread and won't make any more until tomorrow.' Joseph says, 'We've been traveling a great distance. We're very tired, and my wife is hungry.' The baker says, 'Yeah, yeah. I've heard it before.' He hands them a broken cookie. 'This is the best I can do. Now go on. I'm busy.'

"Mary leans against Joseph, she's so tired. Where should they go next?" Elizabeth put the notebook down.

Christy was leaning forward, and Meghan sat perfectly still.

"That's good," said Christy. Meghan nodded her agreement.

"Thanks." Elizabeth let herself enjoy the praise for a moment. "So, what next?"

"What about a store where people are arguing over some presents and the salespeople are so busy they don't even notice Mary and Joseph?" Christy offered, speaking slowly.

Elizabeth nodded and turned to Meghan. "Where's this going?" Meghan asked.

"I thought," Elizabeth twisted a strand of

hair around her finger, "that they'd see a shining light over the church and go there. The minister would say something like, 'You're perfect for the part' and lead them to a stable where Mary will fall asleep. Then the lights dim, and when they come up, baby Jesus will be there. People will come to church arguing about gifts and worried about Christmas stuff, like cooking and wrapping presents. When they see Jesus, they get quiet. Someone reads Luke's story of Jesus' birth, and everyone gathers around the stable."

"Perfect," said Christy. She sank back into the chair, crossed her legs, and kicked the top one into the air over and over.

"So, where else should they go?" Elizabeth asked.

"They should meet a Santa," said Meghan.

"And go into a toy store," said Christy. "Those places are zoos this time of year. Someone has to be trying to find a toy the store's been out of for months."

"What about a bookstore with people buying everything but Bibles?" Elizabeth suggested.

"And a Christmas tree lot with a couple scraggly trees left." Christy glanced at the tree in the corner.

"A post office with people trying to mail packages and cards?" offered Meghan.

"This is going to be great," said Elizabeth. "Each of you write the places you mentioned, and I'll do the bookstore and the ending. I'll give Ms. Clark the list of places and characters ..."

"Who's Mary?" Christy asked.

"I guess Ms. Clark will decide," said Elizabeth. She'd looked forward to being Mary for years, but she knew it wasn't a given. When she gave Ms. Clark the lists, she'd mention how she knew all the dialog and, at this late date, it might be hard to find someone with time to learn it.

"I've been in plays before," said Christy. "Last summer I took a class, and I can learn lines like that." She snapped her fingers.

"It'll be up to Ms. Clark," Meghan said. Christy smiled.

"You done?" Justin asked.

"We've done some work," said Elizabeth,

glad for the interruption. She held up the note-book.

Justin took it and read the pages quickly. "Pretty true to life," he said when he finished. He stood behind Elizabeth and bounced the notebook off her head. "Nobody thinks much about the real meaning of Christmas."

"That's the point," said Elizabeth.

Justin tossed the play onto the coffee table, and Elizabeth smoothed her hair. "Dinner's ready," Justin said.

Christy and Meghan were in the dining room in a flash, with Justin close behind. Elizabeth picked up the notebook and wrote down a few more notes.

"Elizabeth! It's getting cold. What's left, that is," Aunt Nan called. Humming "Joy to the World," Elizabeth joined her friends for dinner.

4
RHYMES FROM THE KIDNAPPER

"Ms. Clark, wait!" Elizabeth caught up with the youth-group sponsor as she was getting into her car.

"I have a luncheon I'm supposed to go to," said Ms. Clark. "Another Christmas thing."

"I have a list of scenery and characters for the play. We'll probably have it written by Wednesday night so we can practice. Depending on how practice goes, we might need a quick practice on Friday night before the service, but I think it's simple enough ..."

"Whoa! That sounds like you're asking people to give up a lot of time. I'm beginning to see why we've always done a live Nativity."

"This is going to be great, though," said

Elizabeth. "And there aren't that many lines for anyone except Mary and Joseph. I'll know all the lines, so I could be Mary and that'll …"

Ms. Clark laughed. "I've already heard this speech this morning, from Christy. She can learn lines like this." Ms. Clark snapped her fingers.

"But I think that I'd do a good job," said Elizabeth, surprising herself with her pushiness.

"I'm sure you would," said Ms. Clark, starting her car.

"Then I'm Mary?"

"I'll let everyone know on Wednesday." Ms. Clark backed out of the parking space and waved at Elizabeth.

"C'mon, Elizabeth," Mom called. "I have things to do."

Elizabeth trudged to the car and got in the backseat. "When are we going to decorate the tree?" she asked.

"Tonight," said Mom.

"I thought we were going to do it this afternoon," Elizabeth said, disappointment washing over her.

"I need to do some shopping," said Mom.

"Presents?" Mike asked. "For me?"

"Okay. I need to do some shopping too," said Elizabeth. She had something for Mike and Aunt Nan. But she couldn't find what she wanted for Mom or Don. Or Justin. She wasn't sure she should buy him anything, but what if he got her something? And Ms. Clark. If I bought her a present, she couldn't tell me I'm not Mary, Elizabeth thought.

"Not this afternoon," Mom said. "I need to do some shopping on my own. There's someone I need to talk to." She smiled at Mike.

"Santa? I bet it is. Elizabeth said she'd help me write my letter, but she didn't. She was watching a movie and wouldn't let me watch with her and Justin."

"Mom, it wasn't a movie for him," said Elizabeth.

"C'mon, you two. Let me get this done this afternoon, then we can decorate the tree tonight. Elizabeth, you'll stay with your brother?"

"And help me write to Santa."

"Okay," Elizabeth said. The thought of an afternoon spent writing a list of action figures didn't fill her with excitement, but she could work on her play afterward.

"Hey, Don's here," said Mike. He rolled the car window down, letting in a blast of cold air, and leaned out, waving.

"You're supposed to keep your seat belt fastened until the car stops," Elizabeth snapped.

Mom turned around and frowned at Elizabeth. "You're full of the Christmas spirit."

"What have we done to get ready for Christmas except run here, run there, rush, rush, rush," said Elizabeth, tears filling her eyes.

"Sweetie, I know it's been busy this year, but it's downhill from here. The giving tree is finished and the gifts divided up for delivery. Tonight we'll decorate the tree."

"I hope there were some presents left over from the giving tree for us," Elizabeth said, wishing she could take the words back as soon as they were out.

"You'll have presents," Mom said, the

warmth gone from her voice. "Don and I are going shopping today."

Don and I, thought Elizabeth, getting out of the car, it's always *Don and I.* Baby Jesus was still missing from the Nativity, and Dolores, their other cat, was curled up in the hay in his place. Elizabeth stood in front of the manger and petted the cat's silky, soft, black-and-gold fur. "Who would take Jesus?" she asked aloud. "Did you see anyone, kitty?"

"The note said he'd be back," Don reminded her. "Besides, Dolores loves it." As soon as he reached toward the cat, she leapt out of the straw and ran to the porch.

Elizabeth shook her head as she climbed the stairs behind the cat. She opened the front screen and would have missed the envelope if the cat hadn't nuzzled it.

Elizabeth picked up the rectangle and saw bright colors peeking through the thin white paper. She pulled out the photo and stared, letting the envelope float to the ground. Baby Jesus, her baby Jesus, sat on the counter at Kirkwood

Bakery with cookie crumbs and red icing smeared all over his cheeks.

"Mom, look!" Elizabeth handed her the photo, setting off laughter in both her mother and Don.

"Baby Jesus is sure getting around," said Mom.

"Who's doing this?" Elizabeth asked.

"Someone with a sense of humor," said Don. "C'mon, Elizabeth, it's funny."

She grabbed the picture back.

"There's something on the back," said Don, twisting his head to see the back of the photo.

Elizabeth read aloud:

> Don't worry 'bout me; I'm still in the 'hood,
> Gobbling up cookies that sure do taste good.
> Waiting and waiting, for the child to be born.
> I'll be back in the nest by Christmas morn!

"A poet with a sense of humor," said Mom, pushing the front door open.

"I'll be right back," said Elizabeth.

"Where are you going?" Mom asked. "I need to leave."

"To the bakery," said Elizabeth. "I'll ask who took this picture and find out who has baby Jesus."

"It's Sunday afternoon," said Mom. "The bakery closes at noon on Sunday, and it's past that."

"Tomorrow then," said Elizabeth. "Tomorrow I'll get him back."

5

SILENT NIGHT

"Is Don staying to decorate the tree?" Elizabeth asked.

Mom nodded and continued to set out the sandwiches she and Don had brought home along with armloads of interesting bags and boxes. "Did you get anything done on your play?" Mom asked.

"I wrote the ..."

"You know this kid is a decent writer," Don said, coming up behind Elizabeth. Elizabeth felt the warm flush that praise set off in her.

"This play has a lot of life in it," Don continued. "You don't mind that I'm reading it, do you? It was sitting on the table and I was clearing it off ..."

"It's okay," Elizabeth said.

Mom had stopped her dinner preparations, smiling at Elizabeth and Don while holding a sub sandwich with lettuce dropping off it.

"I wrote the scene where Mary and Joseph go to the bookstore and everyone is buying everything but the Bible," Elizabeth said. "I still have to do the scene at church."

"Are you writing this alone?" Mom asked.

"Christy and Meghan are doing some scenes too," said Elizabeth.

"Do you have any presents for me under the tree?" asked Mike.

"We might put one or two out after it's decorated," said Mom.

"When are we going to decorate?" Mike asked, whining.

Don pulled on Elizabeth's arm and motioned for her to follow him into the living room. "Your mom didn't give me one clue about what to buy her for Christmas. Do you have any ideas?" he asked.

"You could get her clothes, I guess," said Elizabeth.

"What about something for the house? Anything you need?"

"Not a good idea. I think she'd rather have something for herself," said Elizabeth.

"A book?" Don asked.

"That would be okay."

"I want something *special*," said Don. "How about jewelry?"

"Maybe. Or you could come to church with us," Elizabeth said. Don shrugged.

"Elizabeth, you need to go outside and look at the decorations Don brought over from his house," Mom said.

When Elizabeth opened the door, she had to shield her eyes for a moment, the lights were so bright. At least she acted like she did for Don's benefit. From the doorway, she could see the back of a Santa and what looked like a train.

"You have to see it from the front," said Don, pushing the storm door open. Elizabeth ran to the edge of the walk and turned around. Besides Santa and a train, the entire North Pole was recreated on her lawn—elves, reindeer, candy canes. She rubbed her arms to warm them, then noticed a line of cars slowing to stare at the house. Every so often Santa waved and the train gave a quick toot, toot.

"Isn't it awesome?" Mike asked.

Elizabeth glanced at Mary and Joseph and the empty manger. Too bad Santa hadn't come sooner. Maybe the kidnapper would have taken him or one of the elves instead.

"C'mon, it's too cold out here without a coat," Elizabeth said.

"I thought you might like some animals or something for your Nativity," said Don. "Maybe I can find some this week."

"It's always been enough just like it is," said Elizabeth. No one would even notice the Nativity with all the colors and action on the other side of the lawn.

"These are the best decorations on the whole street!" Mike burst into the living room, letting the door slam behind him. "Look at all the people driving by."

"Maybe we'd better eat *while* we decorate the tree," Mom said.

"All right!" Mike jumped on to the couch, bounced once, and landed in front of the tree. "Lights! First the lights."

"They all work," said Elizabeth. "We tested them this afternoon."

Mike and Don wrapped lights around the tree while Elizabeth and Mom guided them. Elizabeth leaned over the box of ornaments and picked out a cardboard Christmas tree she'd made years ago.

"Wait a minute," said Mom. "We want to do something new."

"New for you," said Don.

"We bought decorations for everybody, and Don will take a picture as you hang yours," Mom explained.

"This is what we did every year at my house," said Don. He handed Mike and Elizabeth each a box.

Elizabeth took hers, feeling unsettled at the change in their decorating tradition. She opened the box and couldn't help but laugh. Nestled in the tissue paper was a Santa wearing a Sherlock

Holmes hat and looking through a magnifying glass.

"Because of the mysteries you've solved," said Mom.

"He's so cute," said Elizabeth. Don had put Elvis Presley singing Christmas carols on the stereo, and she felt her spirits lift. It was Christmas!

"Me first!" said Mike. He hooked a Santa wearing a baseball uniform on the tree.

"Wait," said Don. "I want to take a picture."

Mike stood stiffly and raised one side of his mouth. "Hey, Mike. We looked at bicycles this afternoon," said Mom.

Mike's eyes grew big, and a grin split his face. The camera flashed. "Ouch! My eyes," said Mike. "You looked at bikes, really?"

"Cool mountain bikes," said Don. Mike's smile grew bigger, and Don snapped another picture.

"Okay, Lizzybeth," said Mom.

Elizabeth straightened her sweatshirt and pushed her hair out of her face. She hung her

Santa, then turned and smiled at Don. The way she was feeling, it was easy.

"Beautiful," Don murmured, and the camera flashed again.

Mom took Elizabeth's place and hung a Mrs. Santa wearing a bride's veil on the tree. Don took her picture.

"Now, somebody needs to take a picture of me," Don said, holding out the camera. Elizabeth shook her head. So did Mom. "Somebody has to. Just focus and press this key."

"Too bad Justin isn't here. He's getting so good with a camera," said Mom. "Elizabeth, you do it."

Don picked up a Santa holding a gray cat and hung it on the tree. "That cat looks like Ozzie," said Mike.

"That's why we got the ornament," said Don. Until he'd gotten to know Tiger and Dolores, Don hadn't liked cats. Now he had his own kitten from the litter he'd helped deliver. Mike had suggested the name Ozzie for his favorite baseball player, Ozzie Smith.

Elizabeth looked through the lens, took a deep breath, and pressed the button. It flashed, then whirred as the film advanced. She took another picture. Before she could put the camera down, Mike was hanging ornaments on the tree.

Tiger and Dolores jumped in and out of the boxes of decorations, batting at loose strings and chasing anything that dropped on the floor.

Mom stood by the tree and moved ornaments around. "I wanted that one there," Mike said when she moved one he'd hung.

"It's two red ones together," Mom said. Don and Elizabeth looked at each other and smiled.

When the tree couldn't hold one more ornament, Mom handed Don the angel to go on top. "You're not going to move it, are you?" he asked.

Mom rolled her eyes and shook her head. Don placed the quilted angel on the point of the tree and straightened her skirt. He plugged in the lights, and everyone stepped back to see the finished product.

Mom put one arm around Elizabeth and the other around Mike. Don stood behind them, a hand resting on Mom's shoulder. "Now this is a perfect picture," he said.

Elvis sang "Silent Night," and Elizabeth said a quick prayer of thanks for the sense of peace that filled her at that moment.

6

GINGERBREAD BUT NO ANSWERS

Elizabeth read Christy's department store scene through once, then again, more to give herself time to come up with something to say than because she needed or wanted to read it a second time. She looked up. "This is all?" she asked, leaning against her locker.

"At least she wrote something," said Meghan. "I had to go to my Grandma's, and we didn't get home until late, and I still had homework to do."

"What's wrong with it?" Christy demanded.

"It tells what they're doing, but they aren't *saying* anything," said Elizabeth.

"I figured people could make it up as they went along," said Christy.

"But what if they don't?" Elizabeth asked, thinking about how many people would be watching the play and how a big audience could make even the most talkative person quiet. The Christmas Eve service was always crowded.

"What do *you* suggest?" Christy asked.

"Read mine," said Elizabeth. She handed Christy a copy of the bookstore scene. She'd stayed up late, typing the opening and the new part, planning to add what Christy and Meghan gave her tonight.

Christy read quickly, then tossed the pages back to Elizabeth. She caught a few, but the rest scattered over the floor. Justin and Rich gathered the loose pages as they joined the girls at Elizabeth's locker.

"I hope this is a copy of the math homework," said Rich.

Justin read the sheets before handing them to Elizabeth. "More of the play?"

"Here, read mine," said Christy, giving him her handwritten sheet.

"Don't the characters say anything?" Justin asked. Elizabeth tried, unsuccessfully, to hide her smile.

"I'll bring you the rest tomorrow," said Christy.

"Me too. Promise," said Meghan.

"That'll give me time to type it before we meet Wednesday." Elizabeth straightened the pages, wishing that Christy and Meghan would take the play more seriously. Maybe she should offer to do the rest. No. She shook her head.

"What are you doing?" Justin asked.

"Thinking," said Elizabeth, tossing her hair over her shoulder as if she'd intended to shake it into place, not talk to herself.

"You going to Read It Again?" Justin asked. "If you are, I'll walk with you." Read It Again was the used bookstore where Elizabeth worked after school.

"I'm going to the bakery first," said Elizabeth. "I got another note from whomever took baby Jesus and a picture of him at the bakery. That's kind of silly, because now all I have to do is ask who brought the statue in and took the picture."

"Nancy Drew rides again," said Rich.

"I wish I could go to the bakery," said Meghan. "I'm hungry for one of those Santa cookies with all the icing."

"I'll bring you some of the cookies my mom and I baked yesterday," said Christy. "You'll love them. They're better than any bakery cookie." She looked at Justin, then at Meghan. "Gotta go. My mom will be waiting. We have to go to the craft store to get some more supplies for the gifts we're making."

Making? Elizabeth knew she'd be doing good if she could find time to buy and wrap the gifts she wanted to give.

"I have to visit Mrs. Hanson," said Rich. "I didn't do too good on my math test."

"Me either," said Meghan. "Maybe I should come too."

"Hey, come on. That way I won't have to answer every question. You can have the hard ones." Rich punched Meghan in the arm.

"Promise I'll do the play tonight," Meghan called to Elizabeth as she followed Rich into the math classroom.

Elizabeth zipped her coat and put her mittens on. She stuffed the play into her backpack and slung it over her shoulder. Justin moved his large gym bag to his outside shoulder as he and Elizabeth fell into step. The cold air stung Elizabeth's eyes as they walked outside.

"I think we're going to have a white Christmas," said Justin, his nose twitching as he sniffed the air.

"Saturday it was so warm it was hard to believe it was December," Elizabeth reminded him.

They talked about school and Christmas vacation as they walked downtown. Elizabeth wanted vacation to hurry up and start. There was too much to do to take time out for school. Elizabeth turned into the bakery.

"I'll see you later—or tomorrow," Justin said.

"You're not going in?"

"Better not. I still have some shopping to do." Justin stuck his hands in his pockets and shifted from foot to foot.

"Okay, see you." Elizabeth waved as Justin walked away, his head down and shoulders hunched forward.

A woman she didn't recognize stood behind the counter, talking on the telephone. Elizabeth unzipped the front pocket on her backpack and took out the picture of baby Jesus smeared with icing and crumbs. Her mouth began to water as she smelled the spicy gingerbread cookies spread out on the counter. She could almost taste the sweet cinnamon and tart ginger and feel the sticky raisin eyes as she bit into the head. She counted the change in the zippered pocket of the backpack—more than a dollar. That would buy a gingerbread woman. Elizabeth liked the women better because they had more icing.

"May I help you?" the woman asked as she hung up the telephone.

Elizabeth held up the photograph, and the woman smiled. "That would make a good ad. Did you take it?" she asked.

Elizabeth's heart sank. "I was hoping you'd know who took it. Someone kidnapped our baby Jesus figure sometime Saturday afternoon, and this picture of him was left at our house yesterday. If I knew who took the picture, I'd know who has our statue."

"The picture was taken Saturday or Sunday?" the woman asked. Elizabeth nodded.

"I wasn't working. Reggie would have been here then," the woman said.

"Is Reggie here now?"

"He left last night to visit his family for the holidays."

Elizabeth put the photo away. Disappointment and frustration mixed together, smothering her holiday spirit. "I'll take a gingerbread woman," she said.

The saleswoman tucked an iced gingerbread cookie into a white bag decorated with red and green holly leaves. Elizabeth pushed her change across the counter, but the woman pushed it back. "Merry Christmas," she said.

"Thanks. You too," Elizabeth said.

Read It Again was only a short walk from the bakery. Elizabeth didn't bother to put her mittens on.

Teresa, the owner, had decorated the window with Christmas books, shiny Christmas ornaments, and gold garland. There were people lined up beside the cash register and others browsing among the tables and shelves. Teresa moved from one customer to another, her orange curls wilder than usual.

"Need some help?" Elizabeth asked.

Teresa started, then turned and faced Elizabeth. "I didn't expect you!" she said.

"Looks like you could use my help," Elizabeth said.

Teresa moved close to Elizabeth and shepherded her toward the staircase that rose from one end of the store. "Could you please check on the welfare of my cats? They usually handle visitors well, but today has seen a mass exodus of books bound for Christmas-gift joy."

"Sure, but I could stay here while you go," Elizabeth offered.

Teresa shook her head. "Ascertain the status of their food dish, give them an affectionate pat or two, then rejoin the frenzy of holiday buying." She gave Elizabeth a gentle shove up the stairs.

Elizabeth climbed slowly, finding Teresa's insistence that she check the cats odd—even for her eccentric employer. The stairs gave her a good view of the store. There were even more people than she'd thought. Then she saw why Teresa had hustled her away from the floor.

Justin and Don were huddled with the owner, talking. Elizabeth was fairly certain they were discussing Christmas secrets. She hurried the rest of the way up. No matter how much she wanted to know what was going on *now*, she knew it would be even better to find out Christmas morning. Surprises. She shivered with the thrill. Of course, it was also fun to try to figure out what the secrets were. Elizabeth's spirits started to lift again.

Now if she could only find baby Jesus.

7

CHRISTMAS SECRETS

By the time Teresa managed to get everyone out of the store and lock the door, Elizabeth was exhausted. She had delivered orders to several customers and straightened shelves between deliveries.

Teresa insisted they sit and have a cup of tea, even though Elizabeth knew she should be getting home.

"It's almost Christmas, yet the majority of people seem to have started their shopping today," Teresa said.

"I still have gifts to buy too," said Elizabeth. "I have Mike's and Aunt Nan's, Meghan's and Christy's, but I don't know about Justin. I don't know if I should buy him something."

"Of course you should. You must!" said Teresa.

Elizabeth knew she was on the right track now. "I don't know if he's getting me anything."

"But he is," said Teresa. Then, stirring her tea, she added, "At least, I would imagine he is."

Elizabeth sipped her sweetened tea, watching Teresa's nervous movements over the rim of the china cup.

"Of course, I don't know for certain Justin has purchased a gift, but ..."

"I saw him and Mr. Hamilton here today," Elizabeth said.

"You did?"

"Were they buying a gift for me?"

Teresa took a long drink of tea. She had a collection of china cups and had brought out cups decorated with holly today. "Perhaps," she finally answered.

Someone rapped loudly on the glass door. "We're closed," Teresa called.

"It's Don Hamilton. I've come to get Elizabeth."

Elizabeth gathered her coat and backpack.

"I should help you clean up," she said.

"Charles is coming over, and he'll gladly assist me," Teresa said, speaking of her boyfriend.

"I'll come back tomorrow," Elizabeth promised.

"I'm sure to have plenty for you to do," said Teresa.

"It's snowing!" cried Elizabeth, opening the door and stepping out into the cold.

"They're predicting eight or more inches," said Don. "The parking lot at the grocery store is so crowded, I had to drop your mother off. She suggested I see if you were still at the bookstore, so here I am. At your service."

"Thank you so much." Elizabeth curtsied as Don opened the car door for her. She had to move his camera bag off the seat.

"I have our tree-decorating pictures," he said.

"Already?"

"Those one-hour photo places are great," he said.

"May I see?"

"When we get home," said Don.

Mom was waiting outside the grocery store, carrying two canvas bags of groceries. "It's crazy in there," she said as she climbed in the backseat. "Almost all the milk is gone and I had to buy white bread."

"Yum," said Elizabeth. They always ate wheat bread, so white bread would be a treat.

Don drove slowly through the snow, falling ever more thickly. "It really looks like Christmas now," said Elizabeth.

"How are we ever going to get our Christmas shopping done?" Mom asked.

"It'll be all clear by tomorrow morning," said Don.

"Maybe not," said Elizabeth. "They might call off school."

Don turned into the driveway. Mike ran out of Aunt Nan's side of the duplex. "Do you think we'll have school tomorrow?" he shouted.

"There's only two more days till vacation," said Mom.

"Maybe it'll start early," said Elizabeth. She trudged through the snow that already had covered the grass and the walk. When she pulled open the storm door, a white envelope dropped to her feet. Elizabeth knew what it was without opening it. Baby Jesus sat in the window at Read It Again, peeking over the cover of an open book.

"Look at this! Teresa didn't say a word ..." Elizabeth realized she hadn't had a chance to tell Teresa about the missing statue.

"Is there another poem?" Mom asked. "And come inside. I'm not paying to heat the entire neighborhood."

Don laid his camera case on the arm of the sofa, then carried the groceries into the kitchen while Mom hung up coats in the hall closet.

"There's nothing like a Christmas story ..."

"Louder," called Don from the kitchen.

"Michael get in the house this instant! You don't even have a coat on," Mom yelled.

Mike slammed the door as Elizabeth read loudly:

There's nothing like a Christmas story,
Absent of all blood, not gory,
To bring a taste of Christmas cheer
To all my friends both far and near.
My wandering days will soon be through.
Then I'll return and stay with you.
Though it seems we're far apart,
I always live inside your heart.

Elizabeth felt a surge of warmth as she read the end of the poem. If the person who took baby Jesus knew how she felt about Jesus, then everything would turn out okay. She had to admit, she loved a mystery and had plenty of sleuthing experience after solving a baseball-card counterfeiting, a case of false identity, a cat-napping, and a shoplifting. She was sure she'd figure this one out too.

"Mike, did you see who left this? Did you see anybody?" Elizabeth asked.

"Aunt Nan let me watch TV. I didn't see anything," said Mike.

"Teresa had to see who took this picture," said Elizabeth. "I'll take it to the shop tomorrow and ask her. I wish I'd looked for footprints in the snow, but it's too late now. We've walked over anything that was out there."

"If you can get to the shop," said Don, peering out the living room window. "But how about some pictures you-know-who took." He dug in his camera bag and brought out the tree-decorating photos. Mom passed the pictures to Elizabeth after she looked at them.

"You should have combed your hair," Elizabeth said to Mom, laughing with her about the strands of hair sticking out. "And I hate looking at pictures of myself."

After a glance, she stuck them at the bottom of the pile. "Let me see," said Mike, grabbing the photos.

"I'll have to start a new scrapbook," said Mom, "with pictures of us. Dinner will be awhile. You could start your homework while you're waiting."

She took Don's arm and they walked to the kitchen. Mike tossed the pictures aside and followed Mom and Don. "I'm hungry now. Can I have something? I might faint if I don't have a cookie."

Elizabeth shuffled the pictures again. Don had taken some of her and her friends, and she wondered if they were on the same roll. A picture of baby Jesus before he was kidnapped was mixed in with the pictures of decorating the tree. It was the same size and, she turned the photo over to compare the backs, developed at the same place. The one-hour logo was stretched across the back.

Glancing into the kitchen to make sure everyone was occupied, Elizabeth slowly unzipped Don's camera bag. The rasp of the zipper sounded deafening. She wasn't sure what she expected to find but certainly not her own face smiling at her from a large photograph. She slid it out, thinking it wasn't half bad.

"What's that?" Mom asked. Elizabeth clasped the photo to her chest.

"What are you doing?" Don asked, a slight edge to his voice.

"I was looking for those pictures, you know, the ones ..." Elizabeth's face flamed.

"Lydia, could you go back to the kitchen for a minute?" Don asked Elizabeth's mom. With a puzzled look, Mom left.

Don took the photograph and the camera bag. "This is one of the gifts I'm giving your mother for Christmas," he whispered angrily. "What business is it of yours what's in my bag? You almost ruined the surprise."

"Sorry," Elizabeth mumbled. "She'll like it."

When Don left the room, he took the camera case with him.

8

SNOW DAY

The shrill ringing of the telephone on her bedside table interrupted Elizabeth's dream. Santa Claus was climbing out of a purple van, holding baby Jesus. She grabbed the receiver and pressed it to her ear.

Mom had already answered, but Elizabeth listened. It was still dark outside, so she had a feeling the call meant a snow day. Once the principal confirmed her hope, she hung up and settled back into the warm cocoon of her bed, pulling the quilt up to her nose and wrapping it around her arms. Elizabeth closed her eyes.

A day off. It was always like a gift to get a snow day. Maybe they'd bake cookies. Elizabeth decided she'd wrap presents and work on the play. Her eyes opened. She hadn't written the ending yet. She turned over and closed her eyes again. She had all day now.

Mary and Joseph walked away from the post office. Mary said, "Look, over there. A star."

The scene played itself in her head. Elizabeth turned over again. When the words and pictures refused to stop, she sat up and turned on the lamp beside her bed. Elizabeth started to write.

"What are you doing awake this early?" Mom asked.

Elizabeth looked up from the paper, then around the room. She'd felt like she was in church, celebrating Jesus' birth. It was disorienting to find herself in her flannel nightgown, sitting in her bedroom.

"I came up to turn off your alarm so you could sleep in," said Mom.

"I heard the phone," said Elizabeth. "How much snow is there?"

"Ten inches and still falling. I'm glad I got that bread and milk now."

"Do we have stuff to bake cookies?" asked Elizabeth.

"I think so. Aunt Nan will have anything we don't have."

"Do we have wrapping paper?"

Mom nodded.

"I still need to get some gifts," said Elizabeth.

"Not today you won't. They aren't even clearing the side streets yet," said Mom.

"Then I'll be able to finish the play." Elizabeth threw off the quilt and got out of bed.

"I don't understand you two. If today was a school day, I'd have to blast you out of bed with a stick of dynamite," said Mom, turning to go downstairs.

"It's beautiful!" said Elizabeth, looking out her window at the winter wonderland below. Undisturbed snow covered everything, and the falling flakes muffled any noise.

"I'm baking muffins for breakfast," said Mom.

Elizabeth dressed hurriedly and warmly, pulling her heaviest sweater on over a red turtleneck. She slipped her feet into the fuzzy pink slippers Aunt Nan had given her last Christmas.

Grabbing the play, she ran down the stairs.

"I want to build a snow fort and have a big snowball fight. Then I'm going to build a snow Santa and maybe some reindeer," Mike said.

"It's very cold outside," said Mom.

"I like cold," said Mike. "It's not too cold for me."

Elizabeth took the play into the living room and turned on the computer. She decided she might as well start typing.

The lights on the porch were turned on. Elizabeth stepped over to the window and looked out. The different colored lights reflected islands of blurry color through the snowflakes. The stable was heaped with snow, and Santa wore a snow cap on top of his red hat.

The cats sat at the door, looking at Elizabeth. Tiger meowed loudly. The noise he made when he wanted to go out sounded like "Me out" to her.

"You don't want to go out in this snow," she said to the cats. Elizabeth opened the front door, then the screen. The cats surged forward, but as soon as a flake landed on them, they turned and slunk back into the house. "I told you." Elizabeth said.

She looked out the open door just in time to see a man in a dark coat with a yellow scarf wrapped around his neck and over his face snap a picture of the house. "Hey!" Elizabeth shouted. She stepped out on to the porch and a cold, dampness seeped through the bottom of her slippers.

The man waved and took another picture. Elizabeth ran inside and kicked off her slippers. She grabbed her mom's boots and pulled them on, then ran back outside. At the bottom of the porch steps, she looked up, but the man was gone. Elizabeth stamped inside.

"What were you doing outside without a coat?" Mom asked, pushing the door shut.

"There was somebody out there taking pictures of our house. I'll bet he's the one who took baby Jesus. Maybe I can follow his tracks." Elizabeth grabbed her coat.

"It's probably someone who is taking snow pictures," said Mom, blocking the door. "I'm sure he doesn't have anything to do with the missing baby Jesus."

"You don't know that."

"But I do know that breakfast is ready, and you aren't going anyplace without some hot food in you."

"Mom!" Elizabeth threw her coat on the floor and kicked the boots across the room. Mom sighed loudly.

"Teresa will be able to tell me who took the picture at Read It Again," said Elizabeth. "I'll call her."

Mom placed her hand on top of Elizabeth's as she reached for the phone. "After breakfast," she said firmly.

2
ANOTHER DAY
ANOTHER POEM

Elizabeth typed the last period, pressed the save key, and slumped in the chair. Meghan and Christy had come through with their scenes, and the play was finished. Reaching over, she turned the printer on and typed in the command to print the file.

Elizabeth pushed the chair back, stood, and stretched. Outdoors she could see Justin, Don, and Mike "shoveling" the walk. She watched as Justin and Mike threw snowballs at Don, who seemed to be the only one holding a shovel.

After putting on her boots, coat, hat, and mittens, Elizabeth stepped outside. Immediately, snowballs flew toward her. She shielded her face with her hands. "Not fair!" she yelled. More snowballs flew.

The mailbox was stuffed. Elizabeth took time to pull out the assortment of cards and ads. On top was a plain white envelope, no address, no stamp. Why hadn't she thought to check when she saw the man taking pictures earlier?

Stepping inside, Elizabeth heard Justin and Mike yelling, "Chicken! Get back out here." She'd show them as soon as she opened the envelope to see what the "kidnapper" had sent this time.

Baby Jesus sat in the middle of a display of shirts. Elizabeth recognized the department store where the picture had been taken. She looked in the envelope for a poem. She wasn't disappointed.

> *Got the last shirt without getting hurt.*
> *Another present under the tree.*
> *Aren't you proud of little old me?*
> *Do you miss me a little, a lot?*
> *Perhaps you're searching in the wrong spot.*
> *Where does the spirit of Christmas reside?*
> *Can you possibly find it … inside?*

The bakery, the bookstore, the department

store. Elizabeth looked at the latest photo, then at the pages of the play stacked on the printer. The places where baby Jesus had been photographed were the same places Mary and Joseph visited in the play.

Who knew what was in the play? Mom, Meghan, Ms. Clark, Christy, Justin—anybody who'd listened to her talk in the past few days. Somebody who knew her had taken baby Jesus. But why?

Justin opened the door. "Are you coming out?"

Elizabeth stared at him. "Elizabeth?" Justin opened the door a little wider.

"I'll be out, but you'd better watch your back," Elizabeth said. Justin looked over his shoulder a second time before he closed the door.

Elizabeth tucked the latest picture of baby Jesus between the pages of the play. Maybe she could trick the trickster, but not until she paid back Justin and Mike.

Sneaking out the back door, Elizabeth

quickly packed the wet snow into balls, as many as she could carry. She waded through nearly knee deep snow at the side of the house and crept up behind Justin and Mike as they rolled a large ball of snow across the lawn.

"Justin! Mike!" Elizabeth yelled.

They turned, and she bombarded them with her arsenal of snowballs. They returned fire, running after Elizabeth. She turned and pushed a handful of snow in Justin's face. The three of them ended up rolling around in the deep snow, laughing.

Elizabeth sat up. "It's cold," she said.

"Not if you're working," said Don.

"Why shovel when they expect more snow?" Elizabeth asked.

"We'll never get it cleared if we wait until it's deeper," Don said.

Justin scrambled to his feet and picked up a shovel. He started clearing the sidewalk in front of the house. Elizabeth used her hands to knock the snow off the Christmas decorations.

When she was so cold she was numb, Mom

called them inside, promising hot cocoa. They dropped their coats, hats, scarfs, and gloves in a heap in the hallway, boots piled on the newspaper Mom had spread over the floor. Mom also had built a fire in the fireplace. Elizabeth held her hands out to warm them.

"Get any good mail?" Justin asked. He warmed one stocking-clad foot at a time in front of the fireplace. Elizabeth looked at him, but the question was harmless, and Justin looked like he always did—except for rosier cheeks, chapped by the wind and cold.

"Hot cocoa," announced Aunt Nan, arriving with a tray topped by steaming mugs.

"Marshmallows!" said Mike. "My favorite."

Elizabeth sipped carefully. Don plugged in the Christmas lights and the tree glowed softly, warming the room even more.

"Teresa called," Mom said, joining them. "She said no one has been in today, but she's taking phone orders like crazy."

"Did you ask her about the picture?" Elizabeth asked.

"She said they were so busy, it would be easy for someone to take a picture without her knowing," said Mom.

"So she didn't see anyone?" Elizabeth had been so sure Teresa would have the answer.

"Nope," said Mom.

"You finish the play?" Don asked.

"Almost," said Elizabeth.

"Can we read it?" Don asked.

Again, Elizabeth took a good look at Don but saw no sign of anything out of the ordinary in his face.

"I wrote the scene in the grocery store. Mary and Joseph look at ..." Elizabeth hesitated, trying to make something up on the spot, "turkey. Yes, they look at frozen turkeys and can't figure out what they are."

There was no grocery store scene in the play, but Elizabeth didn't intend to let anyone find that out. In fact, she had a couple other scenes to talk over with Meghan and Christy—scenes that wouldn't be in the play either. But they might make good pictures.

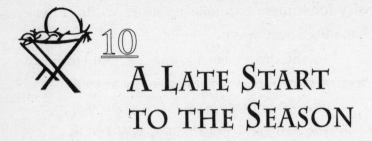

10

A LATE START
TO THE SEASON

School was canceled again on Wednesday, making winter break officially underway.

Elizabeth repeatedly checked the mailbox, the manger, and the front door for a message from baby Jesus' kidnapper. Nothing came.

"Look what I found," said Mom, pointing at the circle of greens in the middle of the table. Three purple candles and one pink candle stood tall among the branches.

"A little late to light Advent candles, don't you think?" asked Elizabeth, taking her place at the dinner table. They usually lit one candle each week in Advent, but this year no one had gotten out the wreath.

"I want to light them," said Mike.

"Me too," said Mom, lighting the four candles. "I've missed our little celebration. It's never too late to prepare your heart for Jesus. In some ways, this snowstorm was a blessing because it's given us time to think about what Christmas is really about."

Mom took Mike's hand, then Elizabeth's. Elizabeth reached across the table and took her brother's hand to complete the circle.

"Father, thank You for my family," Mom squeezed Elizabeth's hand, "and friends and all the blessings You've given us. We ask that You take into Your heart the cold, hungry, and homeless and shelter them from this storm. We thank You for Your Son, Jesus, our Savior, and pray that You would lead those lost in the cold of sin into the circle of His warmth."

Mom looked at Mike. "Thank You, God, for the birds and the food," Mike said and looked at Elizabeth.

"Thanks for my family and friends and all You've given us. Help me follow more closely in Your Son's footsteps." Elizabeth paused, then said quickly, "And help me find who kidnapped baby Jesus. In Jesus' name. Amen."

"Amen," Mom and Mike repeated.

Mom looked at Elizabeth and shook her head. She didn't have to say anything because Elizabeth knew what she was thinking. They quickly ate the chili Mom had cooked and cleared the table.

"Don is going to take you to church," Mom said.

"But I promised Meghan and Christy a ride," said Elizabeth.

"He'll give them a ride," said Mom.

The front door opened, followed by loud foot stamping. "You ready?" Don called.

"Look what Don brought us." Elizabeth couldn't see Mike behind the pile of red- and green-wrapped gifts he was carrying to the tree. She grabbed a couple and put them with the gifts they'd finally wrapped that afternoon.

"You got all these for us?" Elizabeth asked Don as she gathered the play pages.

"They're from my mom and dad," Don said.

"We don't even know them," Elizabeth said before she could stop herself. Immediately, she started to worry because they hadn't gotten any gifts for Mr. and Mrs. Hamilton.

"They're excited to have new grandchildren," said Don.

Grandchildren? Elizabeth wasn't sure how she felt about that. Don had said he wasn't going to try to take Dad's place, so what was this grandchildren thing?

"You'll like them," Don said. "And you'll love their place. It's got a lake and woods. There's even a secret passage in the house."

That got Elizabeth's attention. But she also noticed that Don sounded sad when he talked about the house.

"The passage was used for the Underground Railroad during the Civil War," Don continued, then laughed. "At Christmas, my mom has decorations everywhere, even in the bathrooms. And food. She starts cooking at Thanksgiving and doesn't stop until New Year's."

"You miss her," said Elizabeth.

"It's the first time I won't be there for Christmas—ever," said Don with a shrug. "C'mon, we'll be late. And I won't be driving fast on these streets."

As Elizabeth went out the door past Don, she gave him a quick hug. "We'll have a nice Christmas too," she promised.

Don drove very slowly. The streets had been mostly cleared, but there were a few slick places where the snow was packed. They picked up Meghan, then Christy.

"I'm going to wait for you here," said Don.

"Here? In church?" Elizabeth asked.

"I don't think the carpets will roll up behind me if I walk down the aisle," Don said. "I brought my camera and thought I'd take some pictures."

"That would be nice," said Elizabeth.

Ms. Clark was sorting scenery and costumes as Elizabeth and her friends entered. "It looks great," Elizabeth said, touching the signs that identified each store.

The girls piled their coats in the choir stall. Elizabeth handed Meghan and Christy a copy of the play, then gave the remaining copies to Ms. Clark.

"Who's going to play the different parts?" Christy asked.

"I'm going to pull names out of a hat," said Ms. Clark.

Elizabeth felt her stomach tighten. "But somebody might not want a part," she said.

"Or somebody really bad might get a big part," said Meghan, voicing what Elizabeth was thinking. They'd worked so hard on the play.

"No one *has* to take a part. And Chris Carter is going to be Santa because he has a costume," said Ms. Clark.

The Santa part wasn't what Elizabeth was worried about. She wanted to be Mary. She wished she'd thought to have Mom make her a costume. Or maybe that was a big enough part that no one else would want to take it.

"I thought you had a scene in here at the dance studio. You know, where Mary and Joseph watch *The Nutcracker*," said Meghan, looking up from the script.

"And what about the jewelry store scene—where Mary puts on the diamond ring?" Christy asked.

Those were scenes Elizabeth had made up to see if she'd get a picture of baby Jesus at either store. "They didn't work," said Elizabeth, looking through the clothes people had brought for costumes. There was a beautiful blue robe that she immediately knew would be perfect for Mary. Elizabeth pulled it out and held it against her. The sleeves seemed short and it didn't reach the floor.

Meghan picked up a long blue scarf that matched the robe, draped it around her head, then threw the ends over her shoulders. With her dark hair and eyes, she looked like Mary. Elizabeth held the robe against her shorter friend and realized it would fit her perfectly. Elizabeth and Meghan joined the rest of the youth group sitting in the front pews.

"This is a wonderful turnout considering

the weather," Ms. Clark said. She picked up a yellow plastic margarine tub. "Let's assign parts, read through the play, and get home. I'm going to pick names for the different parts ..."

"Ms. Clark?" Elizabeth interrupted. The woman turned. "Look at Meghan. She's Mary."

"You look lovely, dear," said Ms. Clark. "That costume would fit perfectly, but I'd like this to be fair."

"Does anyone care if Meghan is Mary?" Elizabeth asked the group.

Most of the girls shrugged and shook their heads. Elizabeth looked at Christy whose jaw was knotted, her teeth were clenched so tightly.

"Meghan, it's a pretty big part. Do you have time to learn the lines?"

Meghan's eyes were bright, and her cheeks slightly flushed. "I'd really like to do it," she said.

Ms. Clark's eyes passed over the assembled group, pausing briefly when she got to Christy. "Okay," she said, smiling at Meghan, "it's your part."

Mary and Joseph were Mediterranean, that meant dark hair, not red hair, thought Elizabeth, and Christy's hair wasn't as dark as Meghan's. Meghan would do a good job, and she looked so excited about doing it. In fact, she was already studying the script. Elizabeth decided she wasn't disappointed, not that disappointed. It was what was best for the play.

Ms. Clark quickly assigned parts and passed out costumes. Elizabeth got the part of the baker and a big white hat and apron to wear.

When Meghan read her lines, she slowed her normally fast rate of speech and sounded great. Some of the players sounded like they had learned to read yesterday, others were okay, and some, like Chris, were very good. Elizabeth rated herself okay.

When they finished rehearsal, the parents waiting to pick up their kids applauded. Elizabeth, Christy, and Meghan basked in the compliments they received about the play.

"I can't believe it, but I think this is all going to come together. If everyone promises to memorize their lines, I don't think we'll need that last practice," said Ms. Clark, pushing strands of brown hair behind her ears. "We'll meet here at four to get ready for the five o'clock service on Christmas Eve. Everybody be careful driving home."

Meghan hugged Elizabeth, and Christy threw her arms around both of them.

"It's a terrific play," said Don.

"Thanks," said Elizabeth. It was a great feeling to hear the words she'd written performed. Elizabeth felt so full of happiness she thought she might burst. She didn't quit smiling until she arrived home and saw the empty manger.

11
THE EVE OF
CHRISTMAS EVE

Don drove Elizabeth to Read It Again on Thursday morning.

Elizabeth was beginning to worry about getting her shopping done. She didn't have anything for Teresa, Don, Mom, or Justin, but she had perfect gifts for Aunt Nan, Christy, Meghan, and Mike. Aunt Nan loved music, especially popular music from the World War II era. Elizabeth had found a CD featuring Glenn Miller, a big musician in the 1930s and '40s. Mike was easy. Long ago, she'd run across a St. Louis Cardinals baseball shirt she knew he'd love. She'd bought ballet slipper earrings for Meghan and little gold shopping bag earrings for Christy.

"I'm so glad you're here," Teresa said. She

was behind the counter, ringing up a sale. "I haven't had a moment to prepare these packages for delivery."

The muscles in Elizabeth's neck tightened. She'd planned to ask Teresa if she could shop a while, then work. But the store was full of customers, and Teresa had no one else to help her.

"Charles will arrive shortly to assist me in the shop. He's a master behind the cash register," said Teresa. "He'll also deliver the books outside the downtown area. The temperature is too frigid for you to go far."

Elizabeth took this news as an added disappointment. She wouldn't have a chance to get out of the shop for a while. Teresa excused herself from a waiting customer and showed Elizabeth the stack of books and orders.

"The gift wrap is here and bags here. Write the customer's name and address on the outside and attach the receipt. And if you don't mind," Teresa glanced nervously at the waiting customers, "would you possibly consider wrapping gifts for those buyers who desire it?"

Between sorting deliveries and wrapping gifts, Elizabeth figured she'd be free by New Year's. But she nodded, unable to tell Teresa no.

"Charles! Charles is here," Teresa said as she returned to the counter. Elizabeth heard the relief in her voice. She watched as Teresa took Charles' coat and straightened his tie. They were so cute together.

By early afternoon, Elizabeth had finished sorting all the books that needed to be delivered, including a stack with nearby addresses she could take herself. She'd also gift-wrapped more presents than she'd ever unwrapped. At least books were easy to wrap.

"You dear child," Teresa said, "you haven't had a moment's rest since you got here. Are you absolutely exhausted? famished?" Teresa hugged Elizabeth.

"I'm fine. How about you?"

"Exhilarated! Business is amazing, and ..." Teresa held out her hand. A round diamond sparkled on the third finger.

"Teresa, you're engaged!"

She nodded, beaming. "Congratulations," Elizabeth said, examining the ring.

"It was supposed to be my Christmas gift, but Charles couldn't wait," Teresa said, holding her hand so she could see the ring, then twisting it so it caught the light and sparkled.

"It's beautiful," said Elizabeth.

"Time to return to work," said Teresa.

"Wait." Elizabeth placed her hand on Teresa's arm to stop her. "I could deliver these."

"It's frigidly cold," said Teresa. "I wouldn't consider ..."

"I don't mind. I'd like to get out for a minute." And shop, she added silently.

Teresa glanced toward the customers lining up at the cash register, then at Elizabeth. "Would you mind performing a small favor?"

"I'd love to," said Elizabeth.

"I fear we may be running low on gift wrap," said Teresa, handing her some cash. "See if you can find silver paper, and if you can't, buy any solid color foil."

Elizabeth had worried about the rate she

was using gift wrap too but figured Teresa had more. Teresa handed her some more money. "And would you bring some sandwiches back when you return? Poor Charles—I need to feed him."

Elizabeth bundled up, then loaded the books she needed to deliver in her backpack. "I'll hurry," she said, mentally planning a route that would let her do some Christmas shopping along the way.

The cold air seeped through even the layers of clothing Elizabeth wore. She walked quickly.

At her first stop, the customer gave Elizabeth a tip and insisted she take a bag of cookies too. On the street, people moved quickly, heads down. Their tension and sense of urgency spilled over and washed away Elizabeth's holiday cheer.

She dropped off the second delivery and got a hurried, "Thanks," from the customer but no response at all to her "Merry Christmas." Elizabeth headed toward the post office, dreading the crowd she knew she'd find there.

"Elizabeth! I thought you were working."

Justin was the last person Elizabeth expected to see coming out of the post office. He was carrying the same large gym bag he brought to school every day.

"I *am* working," she said, glad to see him but realizing every minute she talked to him was a minute she wouldn't have to shop.

"Busy?" he asked.

"Unbelievable. In fact ..."

"Yeah, sure. I have stuff to do too. Christmas *vacation*." He shook his head.

Elizabeth waved, then pushed her way inside the crowded post office lobby. A harried postal worker was grabbing parcels from customers and dropping them into a large canvas cart. His face was flushed, and he didn't even glance up as he took the packages from her.

Looking around the lobby, Elizabeth saw dozens of people, each intent on a list, licking stamps, or looking off into the distance. A few tarnished silver garlands and some tinny sounding Christmas music did little to create a festive mood. Elizabeth wondered what people would do if she yelled, "Merry Christmas! Jesus loves you!" Would they even notice? She opened her mouth, but couldn't make herself do it.

Her deliveries finished, Elizabeth hurried to her next stop—the jewelry store. Several weeks ago, she'd seen a mother's ring with a garnet and an emerald already mounted. Her birthstone was a garnet, January, and Mike's was an emerald, May. The two stones were set in a twist of gold, and Elizabeth knew her mother would love it. She checked the window display—the ring was still there.

On the way to the counter, Elizabeth passed a pair of gold earrings—books dangling on delicate gold chains. They were Teresa. Elizabeth pulled them off the rack, then headed to find a clerk to get the ring for her. A few minutes and $54 later, she was on her way to the card shop for gift wrap.

There was no silver wrap, but Elizabeth picked out three rolls of silvery blue and two rolls of red. She had to stand in a line that extended halfway to the back of the store.

Elizabeth looked at tiny Santas dressed in international costumes, ceramic dogs, and picture frames. A large navy leather photo album rested among the picture frames. It reminded her of what Mom had said as they decorated the tree—that they'd have to start a new photo album with Don. She grabbed the leather bound album for him. That left Justin's gift, and she had no idea what to give him.

Looking in every window along the way, Elizabeth headed to the deli for sandwiches. As she stared at unrecognizable camera equipment displayed in the photo shop, someone inside knocked on the window. She looked up and saw Christy waving at her. Elizabeth started to go inside to say hi, but Christy met her at the door, blocking her way.

"What are you doing here?" Christy asked.

"Shopping, working, stressing out because I don't have a present for Justin," said Elizabeth.

"You thinking about something for his camera?"

"Not really. I wouldn't have any idea what to buy. Why? Do you know something good?"

"No." Christy started to walk away from the camera shop, and Elizabeth walked along with her.

"What are you doing out?" Elizabeth asked.

"Last minute Christmas stuff," said Christy.

They reached the deli. "This is where I have to go," said Elizabeth. "See you tomorrow."

"World premiere of our play," said Christy, as Elizabeth went inside.

Elizabeth bought sandwiches, stuck them in her backpack, and headed to Read It Again. Out of the corner of her eye, she caught sight of a window displaying baseball cards. Someone had reopened the baseball card shop! Justin loved baseball cards, in fact, that's what had started their friendship.

As soon as she stepped inside, Elizabeth saw the card she wanted—Dennis Eckersley, one of Justin's favorite players, especially since he'd joined the St. Louis Cardinals.

"Is this the only Dennis Eckersley you

have?" Elizabeth asked the clerk. "Jimbo!"

Elizabeth grinned as she recognized the young man who'd worked for Mr. Becker, the previous owner of the shop. She and Justin had uncovered a counterfeit baseball card scam Mr. Becker had been running, the first mystery they'd solved together.

"Elizabeth, good to see you," said Jimbo. He rubbed his hands together. "What can I do for you?"

The baseball card shop was the first place she'd been all day that wasn't full of people. Good for her, bad for the shop. "When did you open?" Elizabeth asked.

"The day of the storm. I'd hoped to open earlier, but it didn't work out. What do you think of the shop?" Jimbo stood back while Elizabeth admired.

"Great," she said. She had no idea if it was or not, but Jimbo looked so anxious. "I want to buy Justin a present for Christmas. I thought maybe that Dennis Eckersley." She pointed through the glass.

"Justin's been in, and he likes that one," said Jimbo. "He likes this Eckersley rookie card even more." He took another card out and placed it in front of Elizabeth.

"But he's not in a Cardinal uniform," said Elizabeth.

"No, he played for the Cleveland Indians that year."

"I'll take both of them," Elizabeth said.

"I'll throw in hard cases."

The cards took the last of Elizabeth's cash, and she had to borrow change from the lunch money.

"Happy holidays!" Jimbo said as Elizabeth left the shop.

"You too," she answered, smiling.

"You're back!" Teresa said when Elizabeth returned to the bookstore.

"Sorry I took so long. Sandwiches." She pulled them out of her backpack.

"Charles, dear, time for a break." Teresa waved the sandwiches under his nose.

"I wrote a play for the Christmas Eve service at our church," Elizabeth said, then added, "with Meghan and Christy. Would you come see it?"

"How lovely! Of course I—we'd love to, but," Teresa looked at Charles, "we must announce the glad tidings of our impending nuptials to Charles' family. We'll be extremely sorry to miss it."

Elizabeth took off her coat and ran her fingers through her hair. On her way to put her coat in the back room, she passed a display of miniature Bibles. Some had black covers, some white, some red. Inside, the Christmas story according to Luke was printed along with the twenty-third psalm and the Lord's Prayer. Elizabeth chose three black and five white to put with the gifts she'd bought. It would be a small reminder to everyone of the meaning of Christmas.

"I almost forgot," Teresa said. "Charles discovered this on the counter."

Elizabeth took the plain white envelope

Teresa held out. Her name was typed on the outside. She turned it over, then opened it.

Baby Jesus was in a postal cart surrounded by mail—another *real* scene from the play. The tiny slip of paper read:

> *It's the eve of Christmas Eve.*
> *Do you know where your Savior is?*

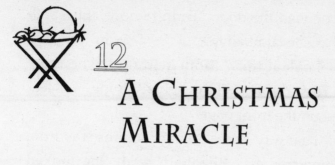

12

A CHRISTMAS MIRACLE

Elizabeth held up the photos of baby Jesus for the young girl behind the counter at the photo shop.

"You want me to tell you who took these pictures?" she asked. The girl wore a holly crown perched on her close-cropped blonde hair and a red sweatshirt that said "Bah! Humbug." She laughed, then pointed at the strips of photos hung along the back of the room. "We haven't had time to breathe, and next week is going to be worse. I don't know who brought that film in. Now quit wasting my time. Next!"

Elizabeth backed away from the clerk, feeling the sting of her words. It was Christmas Eve and baby Jesus was still missing.

Mom waited in the car. She leaned across and opened the door. "Didn't know," Elizabeth said as she climbed in.

"Look at this." Mom held up the newspaper. Their duplex, all the lights shining, was featured on the front page.

"That guy I saw taking pictures was from the newspaper!" Elizabeth said. She looked closely and thought she saw a shadow in the doorway—her yelling at the photographer. "Mom, where's baby Jesus? Who has him?"

"Have some faith," Mom said as she pulled away from the curb.

The church sanctuary was dimly lit when Elizabeth arrived. She wore the white apron over her red plaid skirt and red sweater but carried the hat.

No one else had arrived yet, so Elizabeth sat in the front pew and stared at the cross over the altar. Her mouth felt dry and her stomach all quivery as she thought about the performance. Please, God, open people's ears to Your message and their hearts to Your Son as we celebrate His birth, she prayed. And please don't let me mess up my lines.

The sound of laughter drifted in from the hallway. Meghan, dressed in her Mary robe, entered with Chris Carter in his Santa suit.

"Ho! Ho! Ho! Merry Christmas!" he boomed.

"It's almost time! It's almost time!" Meghan grabbed Elizabeth's arms and squeezed.

Ms. Clark rushed in, her arms loaded with props. "Can you put these where they belong?" she asked. "I have more stuff in the car." She dumped them on the "bakery" counter and hurried out.

Mom and Aunt Nan came into the sanctuary and sat in the front row. Some of the middle rows had already filled.

"You know the part of the play when someone talks about having to take time out from making dinner to come to church?" Meghan asked. Elizabeth nodded.

"I heard someone say almost that same thing as I was coming in tonight."

More and more people streamed into the church, quickly filling the pews. The organist played Christmas hymns softly, but the hum of the crowd nearly drowned out the music.

Ms. Clark gathered the cast, and they prayed together.

The choir, including Mike, filed into the sanctuary followed by Pastor Collins. Elizabeth snuck a peek to see what was happening. She gasped. Justin and his mom were sitting beside Aunt Nan, and Mr. Hamilton sat beside Mom— a Christmas miracle! She was still watching Justin, fiddling with his tie, when Ms. Clark hurried them into place on the altar steps.

Elizabeth played her part, then watched as the rest of the play unfolded. When it was time for the players to go to church, she joined the rest of the cast. Mary and Joseph stood, Mary smiling down at baby Jesus. Elizabeth moved forward with the crowd to get a better look.

She couldn't believe her eyes. It was her baby Jesus wrapped in a blanket that Meghan held cradled in her arms!

13

THE GREATEST GIFT

As soon as the service ended, Elizabeth grabbed baby Jesus out of Meghan's arms, leaving her friend's mouth hanging open. She examined him from head to toe and didn't find anything wrong, not even a chip out of the plaster. Elizabeth hugged the statue to her chest and looked over the congregation. Some people rushed for the exit, but most stopped to greet fellow parishioners, shaking hands and hugging.

People converged on the cast of the play, offering congratulations, compliments, and holiday wishes. Elizabeth smiled and thanked each person who approached her. She was glad to have baby Jesus back, but she couldn't stop wondering who'd taken him in the first place.

Mom was introducing Don, Justin, and Mrs. Thayer to Pastor Collins. Justin kept looking at her, continuing to pull at the knot in his tie.

"Elizabeth?" Meghan tapped her on the shoulder. "I couldn't believe it when I picked him up! Aren't you glad to have him back?"

"Huh?"

"Baby Jesus. He's back."

"Thanks."

"I didn't have anything to do with it. I mean, I'm not really the mother of the Son of God." She held out her robe and giggled. Elizabeth smiled.

"This is for you." Meghan handed her a package wrapped in slick red paper and tied with a gold bow.

Elizabeth stared at the package a moment, then took it. "Thanks," she said again.

"Wasn't that great? Wasn't that fantastic? Wasn't that the ultimate?" Christy put one arm around Elizabeth and the other around Meghan.

"Great," said Meghan.

The photo shop. Christy had been there, and she took pictures. Elizabeth remembered how Christy had hurried her away from the store. Could she have taken baby Jesus?

"I have something for you guys," Christy said. She picked up two green gift bags decorated with plaid bows, then handed one to each girl.

"I have gifts too," Elizabeth said. She found her backpack and opened it, taking out her friends' gifts.

"Let's open them now," said Meghan, sitting in a pew.

Elizabeth tucked baby Jesus under her arm, afraid to let go of him, and sat down next to her friend.

"Mine first," said Christy. "You have to open them at the same time because they're the same."

Elizabeth and Meghan dug through the tissue paper and pulled out a framed picture of the three of them taken at Elizabeth's house earlier in the year.

"I love it!" said Meghan.

"Cute," said Elizabeth. They had their heads together and were smiling at the camera.

"I thought you were going to ruin the surprise yesterday when you showed up at the photo shop when I was picking them up," Christy said to Elizabeth.

"That's why you were at the shop?" asked Elizabeth, mentally crossing Christy off the list of suspected kidnappers.

"What'd you think?"

"Open mine," said Meghan.

Elizabeth and Christy opened the red-wrapped packages. "It's beautiful!" Elizabeth held up a book-shaped locket.

"You can put Justin's picture in one side and yours in the other," Meghan whispered.

"Thanks," Elizabeth whispered, hugging her best friend.

"Thanks. I love it," said Christy, hooking a thin silver bracelet around her wrist. "Now Elizabeth's."

"Oh! Oh!" said Meghan, holding up the golden ballet slippers.

Christy giggled. "Shopping bags. Perfect!"

"Merry Christmas," said Meghan. "My family is waiting. Call me!" She sped away, still wearing her blue robe.

"Merry Christmas," Christy said. "And thanks for all you've done for me this year. Call me?" She moved away more slowly.

"You were great." Mom kissed Elizabeth.

"I was so proud of you." Aunt Nan gave her a hug.

Justin and Don gave a thumbs up at the same time. "You've been spending too much time together," said Justin's mother to her son and Don. "Do you believe the pictures these guys have been taking?"

"Pictures?"

"Tons of them. Some of the silliest ..."

"Mom," said Justin.

"Everybody come on back to the house. Nan baked cookies, and I bought eggnog. I have soup and bread too," Mom said.

"We have to save some cookies for Santa," Mike said.

Justin loosened his tie and hoisted his black gym bag to his shoulder. Why did he have that bag in church? Elizabeth wondered. It looked flatter than it looked yesterday at the post office. The post office, the big bag. Elizabeth looked from baby Jesus to the bag. He would fit. Justin?

Elizabeth and Aunt Nan rode with Justin and Mrs. Thayer while Mom, Don, and Mike followed in Don's car. Elizabeth didn't say much on the way home.

When they reached the house, Elizabeth carried baby Jesus to the manger as everyone else went inside. She removed the envelope with her name on it before gently laying the babe in his bed. As she turned around, Justin had his camera out.

"Stay there," he said, "and smile."

"Did you know this was my dad's?" Elizabeth asked.

"I think I remember you saying something about that." The camera flashed. "One more." It flashed again.

Elizabeth opened the envelope and read:

Wherever I roam, there's no place like home.
I want you to know you've done your part
To convince us that Jesus lives in our hearts.
You've showed us with act, word and deed,
To turn to Jesus when we're in need.

We know that you've prayed that we'd see
His light.
We're happy to say we've seen it tonight.

"You!" Elizabeth said, tears burning behind her eyelids.

"And Mr. Hamilton," said Justin. "Are you mad?"

Elizabeth shook her head. "And do you mean it? Do you really believe in Jesus?"

"Yes," said Justin. "I do. You've helped me see how important Jesus is."

"And you're important to Him too," said Elizabeth. She looked at baby Jesus. "Important enough for Him to be born on earth. Important enough for Him to give His life for you."

The next thing she knew, Justin had his arms around her and Elizabeth forgot how cold it was. They held hands as they walked to the house.

"One more thing," said Justin. He reached in his bag and pulled out a small silver-wrapped box.

"I have something for you too," said Elizabeth. "Inside. Let me get it." She slipped into the house. Mom and Don were standing in the doorway to the living room, kissing.

"Mistletoe," said Mom, pulling away.

"Right," said Elizabeth.

Don pulled Elizabeth over and kissed her cheek. Aunt Nan came out of the kitchen, wiping her hands on a dishtowel, and Don kissed her too.

Elizabeth found Justin's gift, then squeezed past Don and Aunt Nan.

"You'll freeze out there," said Aunt Nan.

"We'll just be a minute," said Elizabeth, closing the front door.

"Here." Elizabeth handed Justin the gift-wrapped baseball cards.

"Let's open them at the same time," said Justin. Elizabeth carefully pulled the bow off, then loosened the tape. Justin just ripped.

"Dennis Eckersley's rookie card!"

"You still like him, right?"

"He's the greatest," said Justin.

Elizabeth lifted the lid off the white box,

then pushed the layer of cotton off. A gold bracelet lay nestled in the bottom layer of cotton.

"It's a charm bracelet," said Justin. "Look, this is a little magnifying glass and this is a blue ribbon and this is a cat. The blue ribbon is for the science fair, the magnifying glass because of the mysteries you've solved, and the cat because you like cats."

"I love it. Help me put it on," said Elizabeth, holding out her arm.

"Can't," said Justin. "Too cold."

Elizabeth opened the door. As soon as Justin came inside, Aunt Nan grabbed him and kissed him. "Mistletoe," she said.

"You two," Aunt Nan continued, looking at Don, then Justin, "gave us the greatest gift of all—showing us you believe in Jesus too."

"Amen," said Elizabeth as the spirit of the season filled her heart.

A Christmas Play

Setting: MARY and JOSEPH enter and walk toward a modern town.

MARY: Joseph, is this Bethlehem?

JOSEPH *(takes MARY's arm):* Bethlehem is much different than Nazareth.

MARY: I'm not sure I want God's Son to be born here.

JOSEPH *(stops in front of bakery):* Are you hungry?

MARY: You must ask? *(Pats her stomach.)*

JOSEPH: We can get some bread in here.
(BAKER decorates Christmas cookies.)

MARY: Those are pretty. What are they?
(BAKER stares in disbelief.)

JOSEPH: We would like some bread.

BAKER: So would everyone else. We're out of

bread. Next batch won't be done till morning.

JOSEPH: We've been traveling a long distance, and we're very tired and hungry.

BAKER: Yeah, yeah. I've heard it before *(hands JOSEPH a broken cookie).* This is the best I can do. Now go on. I'm busy.

MARY *(leans against JOSEPH):* Perhaps in here …

(MARY and JOSEPH enter a department store.)

CUSTOMER 1: That's my shirt. I need it for my father.

CUSTOMER 2: I had it first, and I need it for my son.

CUSTOMER 1: I was in here yesterday, but I couldn't wait in line to pay.

CUSTOMER 2: You should have gotten it then because it's mine now.

(CUSTOMERS 1 and 2 tug on the shirt. CLERK 1 talks on the telephone. CLERK 2 wraps a gift. No one looks at MARY and JOSEPH, who look around and walk out. On the sidewalk, MARY and JOSEPH meet a tired SANTA.)

SANTA *(in a flat voice):* Ho, ho, ho. Merry Christmas to you two. Won't you be glad when this season is over and we go back to wearing regular clothes?

(*MARY and JOSEPH exchange puzzled looks. MARY walks to a toy store.*)

MARY: Look at this. Can we go inside, please?

(*MARY and JOSEPH enter. MARY picks up a baby doll and cradles it.*)

CHILD 1 (*walks along aisle, touching everything*): And I want a fire truck and a gun and a tape player and a …

CLERK 3: We haven't had Oliver the Talking Pig since before Thanksgiving. I'm sorry. No one knew that it would be so popular, not even the manufacturer.

MOM: But our daughter only wants Oliver. We've been everywhere. Don't you have one in the back for emergencies? This will ruin everything. Our whole Christmas is spoiled without that pig.

(*No one notices MARY and JOSEPH. MARY puts doll back and leaves with JOSEPH. They enter a bookstore where people buy copy after copy of slick novels. A stack of Bibles goes untouched.*)

CUSTOMER 3: What do you mean you don't

have a copy of *Kill My Parents, Kill My Kids?*

CLERK 4: We've been out of stock on that since December 1. It's a great Christmas gift.

CUSTOMER 3: What about *The Monster Who Wouldn't Die?*

(CLERK 4 hands over book.)

CUSTOMER 4: I'll take that one too. I'm also looking for something appropriate for a family.

(CLERK 4 holds up Bible. CUSTOMER 4 shakes head.)

CUSTOMER 4: Too thick. Not enough pictures. I want something with a lot of action. What about *The One-Minute Parent?*

CLERK 4 *(holds up two books):* I don't have that, but this one was a movie and this one is going to be a movie.

(CUSTOMER 4 looks through the books. CUSTOMER 3 pushes past MARY and JOSEPH. Leaving, MARY and JOSEPH pass a Christmas tree lot where FATHER tries to bargain for a pathetic tree.)

FATHER: This one has a hole in it. Can't you consider cutting the price a little? I've been out of work, and I'd like to give my kids a tree at least.

CLERK 5: Don't cut the prices for nobody.

(MARY and JOSEPH pass the post office where POSTAL WORKER takes packages and letters.)

CUSTOMER 5: This will be delivered tomorrow, right?

POSTAL WORKER: Tomorrow is Christmas. We don't work tomorrow.

CUSTOMER 5: I thought it was through rain and snow and sleet.

POSTAL WORKER: But not on Christmas.

CUSTOMER 5: This has to be delivered. My mother will think I forgot about her.

JOSEPH *(sits on bench next to MARY):* Everyone here is so busy. They don't have time for two tired, hungry strangers.

MARY: They seem to be preparing for something, but it's not clear to me what it is.

JOSEPH: There must be someplace for us here.

(MARY looks up and sees a cross that looks like a star as it shines over a darkened building.)

MARY: Over there, under the star.

JOSEPH: It looks deserted. Let's go.

MARY: Perhaps there will be a place for us there.

(*MARY and JOSEPH walk slowly toward the light. JOSEPH knocks on the door. MAN answers.*)

MAN: You're here.

JOSEPH: We've traveled far. We're tired and hungry. Have you a place where we can rest?

MAN: Perfect! You are perfect. Come inside. I didn't know what to do when Mr. and Mrs. Brown called to say they couldn't be Mary and Joseph because Mrs. Brown was having her baby. You're perfect for the part.

(*MAN leads MARY and JOSEPH to a simple stable with a manger filled with straw. MARY looks at JOSEPH, shrugs, and curls up to sleep. Lights dim. CHOIR sings a Christmas carol. Lights come up. MARY holds a baby. JOSEPH looks on. CAST enters sanctuary.*)

BAKER: I'm out of rolls. What if someone needs some for dinner tomorrow? All I have left are cookies, and there isn't time to come to church *and* bake another batch. (*Turns to exit.*)

CUSTOMER 1: I hope Dad's shirt is the right size. I still have to finish wrapping the kids' presents.

CHILD 2: Mommy, can I have a doll like hers? *(Points.)* That's what I want from Santa.

MOMMY: That wasn't on your list, and Santa's already left the North Pole.

CHILD: But I want it! *(Stamps feet and pouts.)*

CUSTOMER 4: The reindeer fell over as we pulled out of the driveway, and now the whole scene is ruined. Christmas is ruined. Decorations are what make Christmas.

CUSTOMER 2: I still have to stuff the turkey and stick a pie in the oven. If only we didn't have to take time for church.

(MARY and JOSEPH stand with baby Jesus. CAST quiets.)

MINISTER: On this morning (evening), we celebrate the birth of a baby. We call Him Jesus. He came to a cold, busy, crowded world to save us from our sins.

ALL: Amen. Welcome, baby Jesus.

(CAST gathers around MARY, JOSEPH, and baby.)

The End